THIS BLOOMSBURY BOOK

BELONGS TO

....

TOO PURPLY!

JEAN REIDY

ILLUSTRATED BY GENEVIÈVE LELOUP

BLOOMSBURY

LONDON BERLIN NEW YORK

NOOOOOOOOOOO

Too

PURPLY,

TOO TICKLY,

TOO PUCKERY,

TOO PRICKLY.

TOO ITCHY,

TOO SCRATCHY,

TOO STITCHY,

TOO

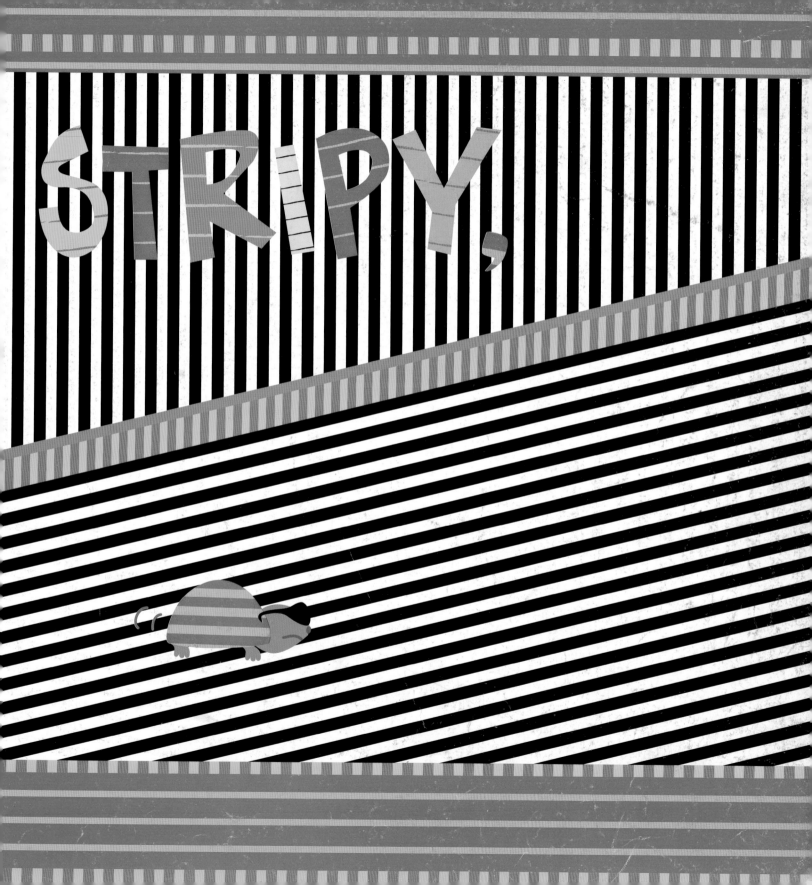

TOO TAGGY,

TOO STRAPPY,

£1

TOO

BAGGY?

TOO FEATHERY,

TOO
DANCEY,

TOO
LEATHERY,

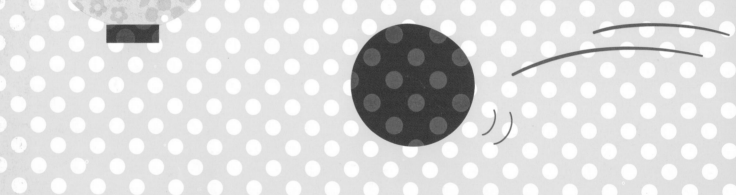

POLKA

SO COMFY! JUST RIGHT.

To Sarah, whose jammies
were always too scratchy
— J. R.

For Lucy, in the sky
— G. L.

Bloomsbury Publishing, London, Berlin and New York

First published in Great Britain in 2010 by Bloomsbury Publishing Plc
36 Soho Square, London, W1D 3QY

First published in the USA in 2010 by Bloomsbury USA
175 Fifth Avenue, New York, NY 10010

A CIP catalogue record of this book is available from the British Library

ISBN 978 1 4088 0315 8

Printed in China

1 3 5 7 9 10 8 6 4 2

All papers used by Bloomsbury Publishing are natural, recyclable products made from
wood grown in well-managed forests. The manufacturing processes conform to the
environmental regulations of the country of origin

www.bloomsbury.com/childrens